Mm

Ll

Kk

Gg   Hh   Ii   Jj

Yy   Zz

Uu   Vv   Ww   Xx

Dear Parent,

The My First Steps to Reading® series is based on a teaching activity that helps children learn to recognize letters and their sounds. The use of predictable language patterns and repetition of familiar words will also help your child build a basic sight vocabulary. Your child will enjoy watching the characters in the books place imaginative objects in "letter boxes." You and your child can even create and fill your own letter box, using stuffed animals, cut-out pictures, or other objects beginning with the same letter. The things you can do together are limited only by your imagination. Learning letters will be fun—the first important step on the road to reading.

The Editors

My "p" Book

(Blends are included in this book.)

written by Jane Belk Moncure

illustrated by Colin King

Little  had a box.

"I will find things that begin with my 'p' sound," she said.

"I will put them into my sound box."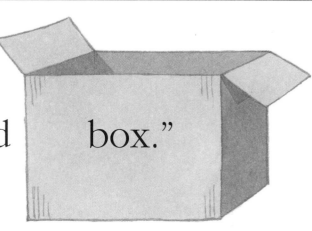

Little 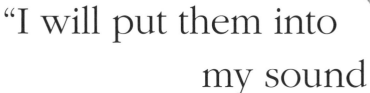 found a poodle

and her puppy.

Did she put the poodle and the puppy into her box?

She did.

Then Little  found a  pig . . .

and piglets  in a pigpen.

Did she put the pig and piglets into the box with the poodle and the puppy? She did.

Little walked down a path to the park.

In the park, she saw a tree with peaches. She put some peaches into her box. Under the peach tree,

Little

saw a picnic table and a picnic basket.

"Let's have a picnic," said Little P.

She opened the picnic basket and found

peanuts  and pickles

and popcorn  and pie.

Little  and the animals ate until the pig said, "I am about to pop!"

Little P put the animals back into her box.

She also put back the leftover peanuts, pickles, popcorn, and pie.

Now the box was so heavy

that it was about to pop!

Then Little  saw a

pony pulling a cart.

"Please pull us!" she said.

The pony pulled them down the path.

They saw a . . .

porcupine.

Little gave the porcupine some popcorn.

She put him into the box . . . carefully . . . because he was prickly.

The pony pulled them on down the path.

Soon they saw a peacock.

Little  gave the peacock some peanuts.

Then she put him into the box.

Suddenly, the pony stopped.

A panther

was on the path!

The pony pranced! The pig, piglets, poodle, puppy, peacock, and porcupine fell out of the box.

The panther pounced

on the box.

He ate up all the peanuts, pickles, peaches, popcorn, and pie!

Then he smiled politely.

Just then, a
police officer
came down
the path.

"You have found our pet panther," he said.
"We will take him back to the zoo."

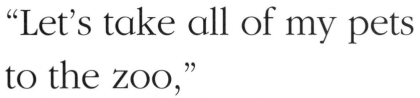

"Let's take all of my pets
to the zoo,"

said Little  .

They paraded along the path to the zoo.

picnic basket

poodle

pony

peacock

porcupine

piglets

peaches

police officer

puppy

pig panther path

Can you read these words
with Little 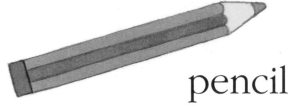 ?

pretzel

pencil

panda

parrot

plane

pelican

puppet

plate

parachute

penguin

piano

Aa Bb Cc Dd Ee Ff

Nn Oo Pp Qq Rr Ss Tt

My First
Steps to
READING®